ADVENTURE IN THE DARK

by Jane Carruth   illustrated by Tony Hutchings

CARNIVAL

Tippu didn't like the dark. Every night he held on to his mother's skirt as they went to bed.

Everyone was soon fast asleep except Tippu. His
night light made shadows on the wall.

Tippu was glad when it was daytime again. But he was having so much fun playing with his new hoop, that he never noticed that nasty Bully Shrew was hiding behind a tree.

Suddenly Bully Shrew snatched Tippu's hoop. ''Catch me if you can!'' he laughed.
''Stop, stop!'' cried Tippu.

Bully Shrew just laughed and ran away with Tippu's hoop. Tippu ran as fast as he could, but he could not catch up with him. He wondered if he would ever get his hoop back again.

At last Tippu lost sight of Bully Shrew. He found
himself all alone in the woods. Then, suddenly,
he noticed that it was getting dark, and he didn't
know how to get home!

Feeling frightened, he tried to find his way home.
Soon it was quite dark, and suddenly the woods were
full of monsters.
''Ooh,'' squeaked Tippu, ''don't eat me, please!''
The giant cat kept quite still.

Quickly Tippu ran away from the monster cat, with its long sharp claws. But behind him was another monster. This one had long horns on its head, and two brightly glowing eyes.
Tippu didn't stay to take a good look. He ran away even faster—but where was he?

In the end he had to admit that he was really lost.
"And I'm getting very tired," he said to himself. "If
I just curl up and go to sleep in the shelter of these
big rocks, maybe the monsters won't find me
here during the night."

He was so tired that he fell fast asleep. Suddenly it was morning and Tufty Rabbit was there. "Wake up, Tippu," said Tufty. "Why are you so far from home?" "I don't know where I am," cried Tippu. "And last night the woods were full of monsters."

"Jump up," said Tufty. "We'll soon be home." On the way they met Tippu's monsters. "Your giant cat was just an old tree," laughed Tufty. "And the other monster was that fallen log, with glow-worms that looked like shining eyes!" Tippu laughed when he saw them.

At home everyone was glad to see Tippu safely back. "We were so worried," said Mummy. Tippu's father thanked Tufty Rabbit for his help.

That evening Daddy took Tippu fishing. "Look,
Dad, they're not really monsters," laughed Tippu.
"Just silly old trees!"

Daddy didn't catch a fish. But he caught something much better! "Hooray!" cried Tippu, and jumped for joy to see his hoop again.

Tippu was sound asleep. He didn't want his light
left on. He knew there were no monsters in the dark.
Pleasant dreams, Tippu!